Algiers:
The Poet's Garden

Palewell Press

Algiers:
The Poet's Garden

Soleiman Adel Guemar

Translated by Tom Cheesman

Algiers: The Poet's Garden

First edition 2019 from Palewell Press, www.palewellpress.co.uk

Printed and bound in the UK

ISBN 978-1-911587-29-3

The following stories: "Batonville", "Black Hole", "Rosa", "Hereafter", "Mama", "Bus Story", "Rendez-vous", "Local Therapy", "Of Stars and Men", "Khobzists, Khobzism", "The Sham", "The Poet's Garden", "The Voice of Reason", and "Criticisers and the Criticisable" were translated by Tom Cheesman, and appeared in the volume *Local Therapy: Stories and Parables from Algeria* (Swansea: Hafan Books, 2013)

The front-cover image of Algiers is Copyright © 2019 Yasmine Belhimer

The photo of Soleiman Adel Guemar was downloaded from https://ainoko.wordpress.com/2010/06/27/illusions-soleiman-adel-guemar/ No copyright infringement is intended

The cover design is Copyright © 2019 Camilla Reeve

A CIP catalogue record for this title is available from the British Library.

Acknowledgements

Sincere thanks to Tom Cheesman for permission to republish the stories by Adel Guemar that first appeared in *Local Therapy: Stories and Parables from Algeria* (Swansea: Hafan Books, 2013)

Dedication

This book is dedicated to all the brave Algerians who broke the wall of fear on the 22nd of February 2019.

Contents

Introduction by Jessica Northey 1

Batonville 7

Black Hole 15

Rosa 17

Hereafter 27

Mama 29

Bus Story...37

Rendez-vous...39

Local Therapy 43

Of Stars and Men...47

Khobzists, Khobzism...49

The Sham 51

The Poet's Garden 53

The Voice of Reason 59

Criticisers and the Criticisable 61

Adel Guemar - Biography..63

Introduction by Jessica Northey

In February 2019 Algeria began the largest, longest, most impressive peaceful movement for democracy, justice, and human rights ever witnessed in Africa, if not in the world. Over the last six months, every Friday, millions of Algerians have marched on the streets in cities across Algeria, and in the diaspora, in a revolutionary movement known as the Hirak. Adel Guemar was there. On the streets, in London where he lives with his family, whilst others marched back home in Algiers. The reasons for these demonstrations are etched into every line of Guemar's beautiful, dark, ironic short stories. Focused on the daily life, dreams and hopes of ordinary Algerians, he paints the hierarchical abuses of power, a tarnished justice system, corruption, disempowerment, violence and torture; but also love, passion and artistic rebellion.

Guemar's stories document how the hopes of the November Revolution of 1954, and the liberation movement that ended colonialism, disintegrated into submission to an authoritarian order. The betrayal of the values of the Algerian Revolution by those who profited, and then abused any who stood in their path, draws us into the history of Algeria and the tragic conclusion of the 1990s 'Black Decade'. Yet the message of the book, and the final story in particular, is more complex. The story of the *Criticisers and the Criticisables* alludes to a deeper problem which might include us all: that of the implication of more than just the elites. The 'criticisables,' who we assume are the ruling class, might dominate the 'criticisers', the ordinary people, he writes – but the ordinary people themselves can fall into the 'criticisable' class. The line is blurred between those who profit from the system – known as the *Khobzistes* – and those who suffer under it.

1

The violence of the 1990s in Algeria touched the whole population. From the soldier, killed for meeting with his love — the fate of Fatima and Ali in the *Rendezvous* — to the artists, poets and journalists. The metaphorical death of the journalist in *The Voice of Reason* is less violent than that of the poet, as he reins in his free will in self-censorship and accepts a mundane existence and verbatim reporting of official press releases at 'The Gentle Citizen' newspaper. The rejection of beauty and creativity in *The Poet's Garden* and the mob hysteria that leads to the poet's death, takes its toll on the mob, so many of them dying along the way. Yet the garden remains, and there is a glimpse of hope as "the young boys played at being the little poet."

The violent repression of opposition voices in the assassinations of the *Black Hole* and *Hereafter* could be the 1990s, just as it could also be the War of Independence, when the colonial regime executed and tortured in an institutionalised system of violence documented so clearly in Henri Alleg's book *The Question*.[1] Guemar's protagonists die with humour, honour and courage. They deny the torturers the pleasure of their suffering. In *Hereafter*, on death row, Guemar's protagonist announces: "I was determined to stay healthy, in body and in mind, for the execution. After all, it was my execution, the only one I was ever going to have!"

I am writing in Algiers, September 2019, after an intense week teaching doctoral students in Jijel, in the east of Algeria. I have

---

[1] Henri Alleg, *The Question, (London, 2006 [1958])*

worked in Algeria since 2007, both living in Algiers and then travelling back there many times to conduct my doctoral research. Only recently, I discovered Jijel, a region which suffered immensely in the violence of the 1990s. The city has many stories to tell. It is a place of history, and of multiple migrations of different populations, cultures and empires which have ruled across the Mediterranean to the current day. From Phoenicians to Romans, Arabs and the French, it was also the site where the Ottomans entered Algeria. Landing in Jijel, the Ottomans conquered the Spanish in neighbouring Bejaia, and went on as far as Tlemcen, fighting aside the Algerian elites and the *grandes familles* whose descendants still play an important role in intellectual life and Algerian civil society today.

The multiplicity of identities resulting from this rich Algerian history is now at the forefront again with the Hirak movement as Algerians strive to stay united. As I write, the political actors of the Algerian elite, the army and civil society continue to negotiate a complex form of dialogue, to engage in a meaningful transition, away from the corruption and nepotism which has prevented this vibrant and intelligent society from truly advancing. The new roads, universities, ministries and the largest mosque after Mecca and Medina, all built in recent years, are impressive. But it is the opportunity for social development, intellectual freedom, justice and the rule of law that Algerians really want.

Guemar's stories paint the perfect picture of all these challenges facing Algerians – ones which were there when he left to claim asylum in 2003 and which remain today. It is about these challenges that young Algerians are now demanding responses, as they march every Friday, week in and week out. This was at the heart of discussions with the students in Jijel this week. The rule of law and democracy are somehow entwined in the debate around identity and language, as young people seek to understand their place in the world. Algeria is transitioning towards English as a language of education: a goal I know she can most certainly achieve, given the talented multilingual young people with whom I have spent the last week. Yet, I hope it is done with care and over time, taking into account the need to nurture those destined to review once again their language of instruction. It must also protect the heritage and memory of the francophone artists and writers who make up this complex identity and who deserve recognition as well. Guemar writes in French, as do so many Algerian writers of his generation, who were often forced, as the great Algerian writer Assia Djebar, into exile. Djebar herself criticises the stultifying effects of the post-independence language policy, which seemingly banished Algerian Arabic and lead to the exile of so many Francophone writers. She describes how "the denial of an entire people's genius went hand in hand with mistrust of a minority of French-language writers whose production, (...often) continued in exile.[2]

Returning to Algeria, with the Guemar family this year, I realise the importance of these current debates and the huge political transition the country is grappling with. I realise the importance of

---

[2] Assia Djebar, *Algerian White* (New York, 2003). Originally published by Albin Michel S.A., Paris, France, in 1995, under the title *Le Blanc de l'Algérie*, p. 228.

Guemar's writing and his message. Guemar overcomes the language divide, and eloquent translations of his work into English and Arabic open it up to all Algerians and to those who want to learn more about this important country. Whilst the bitter experience of the 1990s and the harsh legacy it left behind remain the burden all Algerians have to bear, and overcome, both mentally and physically. There are many traces of hope in Guemar's work. This hope is also reflected in the huge optimism on the streets, in the university I have just visited and in homes across Algeria, despite the fears and caution they must also carry. The crushed hopes of utopian idealists have given way to a more pragmatic vision. There is now a realisation that a better Algeria is possible and that Algerians must strive together to achieve it. The incredible Hirak movement since February 2019 has transformed Algerian politics forever. It is fine to have doubts and caution. This might even be a necessary good. But as Guemar writes in *Of Stars and Men,* we still need to look to the stars, as well as to men. He concludes, "time, fraying at the pace of the sufferings of passers-by, scorches their hearts and crushes their huge eyes. Might they then, perhaps, doubt a little? So what! So long as there are stars and men."

Batonville

First one makes others tremble, but then the others end up infecting you with their terror. This is why tyrants too live in horror. (E. M. Cioran, History and Utopia)

Since dawn the population had taken over the pavements of the main road in Batonville. Pathetic scenes abounded. Impotent old men dragged themselves at all costs towards the gathering-place. Pregnant women, already on their feet for hours, were clubbed down by the leaden sun. But all had turned out to welcome Si-Sercomi, the division's new regional commissioner. And all their hearts swelled with hope.

Hard labour had gone into making the town rise to this occasion. Sercomi was known to be asthmatic and prone to fits of rage. So the palace, which was to accommodate him had been moved, block by block, close to the woods on the edge of Batonville. Enormous cranes and special helicopters made in Taiwan had not been too much trouble.

Reconstructing the giant puzzle of concrete, XC-35 carbon steel and Chinese crystal (manufactured under licence) had taken the masons and architects of Batonville a hundred times longer than would have been required to build a school with ten classrooms. (The association of retired accountants would later confirm that the operation had also cost a thousand times the price of ten such schools.) But the trickiest part was finding a fast and above all efficient way of eliminating the nearby slums.

Following three consecutive days of stormy discussion, often culminating in physical combat, at last the decision was taken to use a large red felt-tip pen. The huts were erased from the map of the town and dynamited, along with their occupants, the following night. What remained was crated up and sent abroad as 'export of raw materials.'

And when at last the town was ready to welcome Si-Sercomi, the population needed little convincing: "Those present will be entitled to a colour photograph of Si-Sercomi! All others may prepare to spend the rest of their lives laying roads in the desert." So decreed the high committee for surveillance and security on Radio Baton.

Rumour had it that Si-Sercomi was not like his predecessor, Sambiti. Sambiti was without pity. When he was in a bad mood he would announce a curfew in the poor neighbourhoods and pace around, brandishing his cocked revolver, shooting anything that moved. To a close collaborator he said one evening: Fassal, my dear friend, let me check whether you've got anything other than cowshit in that ugly skull of yours. – A test? Oh yes, boss, I love tests. – Right then. What do you reckon is the best sport in the world? – Eating, boss! – Try again, idiot! – Er, dunno, boss. – Think. – I am thinking, I just can't work it out, boss. – Pigeon-shooting, idiot! – But, boss, there aren't any pigeons round here. – One does what one can, dear Fassal. One does what one can.

They were alone in this bar (and Sambiti was in a bad mood). He had just killed all the customers, one by one, sparing only the barman and a prostitute who was too thin to make a good target.

The notables of Batonville were just as much in fear of Sambiti's rages. He would enter their houses unannounced and request the use of their wives and daughters to play with. There was no negotiating these loans. Everyone knew, though, that he was incapable of playing for more than an hour or two. And besides, Sambiti protected them from the cruel taxman. So they were in his debt, whatever they might have said later.

But just as the weather has no respect for persons, Sambiti had ended up old and myopic. In fact he became a laughingstock. People no longer hid when the old fool went out shooting pigeons. He couldn't hit a cow at five metres.

No regional commissioner of the division in living memory had suffered such humiliation. The cows strutted carefree in the streets of Batonville. Dogs roamed about, pissing openly at the foot of the high walls around the villas of the slipper-clad notables, who dug themselves in, waiting for better times. And fearing that the example set by the animals might corrupt their children, every night when they put them to bed they made them repeat: "The animals have nothing to lose. We do!"

Alerted to the gravity of the situation, the staff at division headquarters met urgently, analysed the facts in the light of the latest socio-political theories, drew up each member's horoscope and decided unanimously to relieve Sambiti of his duties. "He's not up to it," was the murmur in the corridors of division headquarters. Sambiti was promoted to plenipotentiary ambassador and Sercomi became the new regional commissioner of the Batonville division.

Since dawn the propaganda service's loudspeaker cars had been trawling through Batonville in every direction, emitting frenetic vocalizations over a backdrop of festive music. The crowds crammed onto the pavements listened very attentively to the divisional commands, and came out in goose-pimples.

(One man: he was among the first to arrive. This sort always stayed clearly in view. He hoped to obtain a colour photo of Sercomi. Maybe even two! Some got three in one month! Such are always the first to arrive, to applaud, to keep quiet.

One child: he sneezed so powerfully that he got two massive slaps on the face. Another smothered sobs in a patched handkerchief.

A farmyard: hundreds of cockerels, no one knew where they came from, leapt into the crowd, submerging the forces of order for interminable seconds. This incident seriously worried the division's secret services, and even to this day they still maintain that hostile foreign agents were culpable. But in fact the cockerels had responded to the appeal of their subversive instinct. And as soon as the crowd had shed its goose-pimples, the cockerels vanished into the landscape, leaving just a few feathers behind.)

The division's recommendation to the population was this: never dream outside the framework of the law; avoid anarchy by practising self-discipline. Policemen took down the names of late-comers, kicking them in the buttocks. "Sercomi, Sercomi," the crowd chanted impatiently. So loud they shouted, some old codgers even passed on before the appointed hour, so missing Si-Sercomi's historic entry into Batonville.

Empty-eyed, expressionless, Sercomi, but for the moustache, was the spitting image of Sambiti, seen in profile. His official assumption of duties was marked by a hand-kissing ceremony. This in itself was already a radical break with his predecessor's anti-hygienic practices: Sambiti had marked each anniversary of his nomination with a foot-kissing ceremony. Deeply moved, the notables of Batonville praised this initiative in their newspapers as a "great step forward" which was both "authentic" (sic) and "concrete proof, beyond any doubt, of a real determination to bring about change!"

The survivors of the Sambiti era were, then, witnessing events without precedent in the annals of their town. Great intellectuals emerged from the pullulating magma in which Sambiti had so cruelly confined them. The postman brought each of them the "Glorioule" medal, Batonville's supreme distinction, which automatically opened every door to them, notably those of radio and television, on which henceforth they were to lull the population all day long with recitations of their speeches and their authentically Batonesque, pedagogically crafted explications of Sercomian philosophy.

Loulou Bentoutou, empirical doctor in material resistance, famed for perfecting the humidified titanium wire brush, provides a perfect illustration of the tragedy of this misunderstood generation. Enjoying a rare moment of relaxation in the depths of his laboratory one day, Loulou had the brilliant idea of composing the following lines of verse: "Sercomi comi-comi djabenna triciti mabine lila oun'har / Sercomi comi-comi H'na maâk l'itirniti Oulli mayh'abakchi maghiar!"

Which means, more or less, this: "Sercomi double comi, you installed our electricity overnight / Sercomi double comi, we support you for all eternity, and those who are against you are nothing but jealous!"

The moment these verses were broadcast from Bentoutou's oral orifice, the special services (subsection internal audio-surveillance), who had encrusted every wall in Batonville with high-fidelity preventive hearing aids, set about decoding the overheard text, and its unheard-of subtexts too, of course.

Weighing in at one hundred and fifty pages, their conclusion, deposited at the office of Sercomi's faithful collaborator Lassaf, was shining: "Loyalty beyond all suspicion (...) Exceptional individual (...) He was born here, we can trust him (...)"

Loulou Bentoutou was appointed pronto to be director of information and cultural affairs for the regional commissioner, who ordered that the poem in question should be chanted in chorus every morning by all schoolchildren in Batonville, straight after the national anthem and the raising of the flag.

Batonville could breathe at last! People came and went at will. Lights out, fixed at 9pm, was put back an hour. Everyone thanked Sercomi for keeping his promises. And by way of proof of his good faith, he even forbade his men from employing the repressive and humiliating method of kicking people in the buttocks with their boots. Nor indeed did he permit any method other than the so-called "slap", whereby the head, seized by the hair – slaps usually being administered also to the face – is buffeted by a series of blows with the back of the hand. "Best way to put some colour into doleful faces!" as Si-Sercomi put it at a press conference. After three weeks of this intensive care, the inhabitants of Batonville all had pink cheeks.

Sercomi now leant his support to light industry. He encouraged the manufacture and promotion of muzzles. These were soon to be found everywhere: at the baker's, the butcher's, the hairdresser's and even the bookshop. Immense muzzles were painted on walls by great local surrealist artists. And above each fresco, this motto: "Words untold, silence gold!"

The muzzle business flourished increasingly, and in time Batonville became the most silent inhabited region of the earth: one of the leading centres of meditation, sought out by countless casualties of noisy western civilization as the perfect place to exorcise their anxieties.

"The only liberty is the supreme interest of the people!" raged Si-Sercomi in his palace. He took his binoculars, went onto the balcony, and addressed Lassaf and Loulou Bentoutou: "Look at them all! Aren't they adorable? What do we do with anarchists? Twist their necks, so!"

A few back-streets away, under the rotting wooden bridge which divided Batonville into two distinct areas, three urchins in rags stripped off their muzzles and threw them into the water among the poisoned fish, the dead dogs and the strangled cats. Phew! And shit! Pass the dynamite!

Black Hole

My dreams dissolved little by little in a specially prepared tank of hydrochloric acid. My eyes melted away, followed by my skin and hair. I just had time to see the sun pierce the rusty metal bars on the window and disappear into my black hole. At least the attempted trepanation a few days earlier hadn't been totally pointless. Original, to see oneself burned and feel no pain. I smelled the scorching and the acid. I knew they were really pissed off that they'd let their pseudo-specialists have a go at my brain before they'd had a chance to play torturers. Ah they hoped so much to enjoy the sight of me suffering! That ecstasy was not to be had this time, too bad. Anyway I know they won't make the same mistake again. The next victim will no doubt be burned alive without anaesthetic. It's too cruel. Luckily I still have those bits of my dreams that haven't been completely annihilated. It's true: everything's relative. I expect I'll see what it's the reverse of when I get to the other side…

I don't know how much time has passed since my last public speech. Days, months, even more… But I do remember people were happy to hear me say what they'd been thinking for so long. Their faces shone. You'd think I'd promised them the moon. But it was total hysteria when one young man in the crowd shouted: "They'll all burn along with the mountains of money they stole!" Another answered: "In this world, not the next!"

Fists clenched, children beat their breasts, like American Indians, Apaches, Sioux and other Comanches preparing for war against the Yankees. The women sang revolutionary chants and ululated stridently. Some of the men looked around with challenging expressions. You'd think they were tuned to the secret radio waves of the lobotomised mercenary herd who, a few minutes later, slashed the stupefied crowd apart with a tsunami of stun baton blows and tear-gas bombs.

Me, I didn't really have time to be surprised. Rifled-butted down and thrown pronto into the boot of an unmarked car that drove for a long time. Its shock-absorbers were kaput. The humpback bridges cracked my skull. That's all I remember. That's all I have to say for now. Look after yourself!

"Don't worry, be happy!"

Rosa

1

The one window of the tiny room I've rented looks out onto a scruffy lane, notorious for its dodgy corners. At night, sleep is impossible. One must wait for the first glimmer of dawn, after the infernal crashing of the bars' grilles being lowered, and for the dogs, which live in fear of everything that moves, to become too exhausted to bark out any more of their bizarre supplications. Even then, the rapid exchanges of the *mouadens*[3] continue in fits and starts for another half hour before their voices fall away into long, deep, quivering sighs. The variety of sounds specific to the depths of night will always amaze me. The coughing fits of tubercular beggars mix with the yowls of cats contesting ownership of a passing female. And in the distance, the murmurs of waves washing the rocks of the port shush indistinctly, persuasively. One moment more and at last all is silent.

It's a month now since Rosa left. I still have the handkerchief I took off her that night in Tala-Guilef, in the hotel at the foot of the Djurdjura.

The receptionist bent himself double. He was not being obsequious, no, that's how it always is. Seeing her for the first time, all men feel an agreeable sharp chest pain. All are tempted to drop everything and follow her to the ends of the earth. And

---

[3] Mouaden: Algerian form of "muezzin".

since she is always smiling, albeit a sad smile, and her eyes are profoundly limpid, all resign themselves and dare to go no further.

2

First floor, room sixteen, stammered the receptionist. The balcony looks out over an empty swimming pool. Snow lies everywhere. Rosa flings her jacket and jumper down on the rug and throws herself onto the bed. It took us four and a half hours to get here from Tala, our neighbourhood in Algiers, due to the slippery road and the police roadblocks.

With damp hair she's lovelier than ever. It's the first time, every time I take her in my arms, let down her hair, and we make love.

I realise she can give other women complexes. They must feel ugly, twisted, superficial, in her presence. Chabha's animosity towards her is particularly fierce. She calls her a slut, a tart.

3

When I met Rosa she was still at *El-Journal*, a large circulation daily. She worked in the advertising department. One day, when I was in a fix with two articles to finish for the following day, she offered to lend me a hand. That evening I had to take her back home. Not long afterwards she left the paper, having thrown an ashtray at the editor's head. "He thinks he can get away with anything, just because he got me that flat. It's only a miniscule bedsit in a crappy part of town. I thanked him and everything, as you do, but he still keeps on at me. It's not as if I was ever going to sleep with him!"

After that she never stopped travelling. Journeys are her great passion: to go further, ever further. She never failed to keep in touch with me. Once, she was away longer than planned. I waited at her flat for five weeks. Ramdane visited every weekend he could. He was in the middle of his exams. He told me about his courses, I told him about the newspaper. And we had fun cooking: onion and parsley omelettes, mostly, or spaghetti in tomato sauce. On other days I heated up the meals she had left in the freezer for me.

When the war ended there was serious friction in Rosa's family. Her father had died in the resistance, her mother wanted to leave, and the family wouldn't let her take Rosa with her. "We don't want her turning into a *roumia*.[4]" And her mother left.

When she was seventeen, the family decided to take her out of school and marry her off to a rich cousin. She wept for nights on end until resignation gave way to a kind of nervy excitement. The feverish wedding preparations gave her a vague feeling of being happy. Her aunts lavished all their last pieces of advice upon her, everything a young virgin needs to know by heart. Then the great day came, summer, the descent into hell.

4

For nearly a year I endured the worst cruelties. At eighteen years of age I'd had enough for fifty! He's out of his mind. He gave me such a rough time! And his mother, a real witch, she took great

---

[4] Roumia: foreigner, specifically European or French. The Arabic term is derived from "Roman"

19

pleasure in seeing me with black buttery eyes and bruises on my face. He used to make love to me like an animal. By night-time he'd be dead drunk, vomiting everywhere as he came to bed, then forcing me to kiss him on the mouth. To prove I loved him, as he said. To think I might have had a child by that monster! He never stopped screaming at me that I was nothing. Nothing but the daughter of a *roumia*. Then I'd remind him it was my father who'd died fighting, burned alive by napalm, while his was twiddling his thumbs as a border guard. I'd say that while I protected my face. I'd stopped being scared of his blows.

Hadj Benkbir, his father, a notorious businessman, was famed for his generosity. He used to make donations to fund the construction of mosques. At the end of Friday prayers, mobbed by the local beggars, he'd sing the praises of charity. He'd make his way home with his right hand inside his jacket, under his immaculate gandoura, taking out clinking coins and distributing them – never counting them – to the indigent crowd, who'd shower him with their generous blessings. Fair return. Everyone saw in Hadj Benkbir the living embodiment of piety – "God bless him!" – all except me, of course, who knew it was nothing but a great, vulgar masquerade. "Just look at that face, lit by the seal of faith!" Embellished with a meticulously trimmed white beard, it was the face of nothing but an august crook.

He owned a dozen shops and immense tracts of agricultural land, but his income didn't make him lose his head. He always remembered the horrors of the 1940s food shortages. Yet he did deviate slightly in two respects while I was staying with them: a black Mercedes for himself, and a white one for his son and sole

20

heir. The latter was especially proud of his. Proud, too, of owning his own restaurant, and a hotel as well.

His favourite game was to tell me the story of the war, while he was giving me one. I got the impression he was fighting his own little war against other people, against the evil eye. His real heroes were the last-minute recruits to the cause, the dandies, the skivers, and to hell with the hardliners, the real lads! He'd learned his lessons well! You couldn't blame him, he'd just never learned to see further than his cash register. He was only echoing his elders, who'd grown fat on this chaotic prosperity. He thought I'd never dream of leaving him, orphan that I am. But as you see! I'm my father's daughter. I threw it all away and moved in with a girlfriend, a student, in university accommodation at Bab El-Karma. I began divorce proceedings, and I waited. I worked part-time as a nanny for a lecturer. She paid me three thousand dinars a month. Luckily I had some jewellery. The bank gave me a tidy sum for it, four million. My lawyer wouldn't give credit. He kept telling me that divorce cases usually drag on. I just wanted to get it over with. Meanwhile the friend I was staying with got into serious trouble because of me. I'd rebuffed the advances of a senior administrator. So they remembered a clause in the regulations banning non-students from university accommodation.

I waited a few days and went back to my lawyer. He asked for more money, then advised me to be patient. I hit him in the face with my handbag and slammed the door behind me.

5

I've always loved listening to Rosa talk. I smile. I say nothing. That night, in Tala-Guilef, we wrapped ourselves up warm in our pullovers and walked arm in arm along the path around the hotel lit by the flickering halos of lamps.

Our steps crunch in the snow, which is still falling. Our breath forms a mist which instantly vanishes, snatched away by the night. I want daylight to never return, and Rosa beside me singing a thousand-year-old song.

Frozen and trembling, we are welcomed by the young receptionist's handsomest smile. The warm air indoors reinvigorates our bodies. Rosa's cheeks and nose are red. She wipes her hair with a handkerchief which she throws in my face.

– Did I tell you Ramdane came to see me?

– Is he better?

– Dark ideas… head full of dark ideas.

– Wanting to change the world… that's him.

She jumps from the bed onto the chair, from the chair onto the bed, making the springs squeak.

– Got you!

The moon cuts a crescent from the sky, glinting on the window while wolves howl in the dark distance. The more I watch Rosa sleep, the more I realise what crap destiny is and how stupid people are. She is always jolted about by the same dream. A nightmare. She's being chased by men armed with axes, accompanied by bald women baring their claws. She's starts to cross a railway line when her foot gets caught. She falls. She can't free herself. In the distance, a train whistle blows. It's coming. It's coming at speed. Rosa's forehead is wet with great drops of sweat. I wipe her face with my hand and kiss her. The train stops. Exhausted, the horde behind her stops, but they will set off again, charging after her, in a moment, Rosa will get her foot caught in another rail and the train will whistle again. I feel her body shake under the covers and I think of all the mad things she may have done.

6

A year had gone by since I'd filed for divorce and still nothing had happened. My lawyer had sent me a new bill, accompanied by a letter saying that he'd been profoundly shocked by my negative behaviour. I'd told myself he must still be hopeful. I must have really got up his nose, the bastard. My friend the student had mentioned a cousin of hers, a senior magistrate. "Mention me. He won't make any demands on you," she'd said. I put on my glad rags and went to see him.

On hearing my story he pursed his lips and said that alas, the machinery of justice grinds all too slowly, sometimes it breaks down, but always it resumes its solemn march in order to arrive, inexorably, at last, at the truth. Ouf! Never despair! And so? What's the answer? Really, there's nothing he can do. It's a banal matter which will take its inevitable course. He hadn't taken his eyes off my cleavage once. His comfortable brown leather chair swaddled him. A respectable old bloke, padded with best quality fat, he was starting to slobber! What's the answer? There must be one. So I agreed. He couldn't help but bare his blackened teeth in satisfaction. I could tell he drank whisky by the litre and smoked big genuine Havanas.

We went to a luxury villa by the seaside and he did all he could to perform. A week later I got my divorce. My friend the student was delighted for me. Most helpful, her uncle or cousin or whatever he was.

7

The next morning Rosa and I climbed up to the Laïser plateau, about two miles from the hotel, then we walked on as far as Lake Goulmine. We had fun making holes in the thin layer of ice which covered it – there were no stones, so we threw chunks of ice, hard as granite. Above our heads there were few clouds, mostly catching on the lower peaks or blown by the wind towards the plains. Rosa wiped butter over her lips, on my advice, to prevent chapping.

I stretched out on the ground and she threw little snowballs at me. Her red hat fell off two or three times, and her hair whirled in every direction. She came and lay down beside me and we ate bits of snow, which tasted like chilled resin. I tried to take off her sunglasses but she wouldn't let me. She struggled with me while she tidied her tousled hair.

"Your hat! Where's your hat!" A gust of wind had carried it off into the middle of the frozen lake. A red dot on the crystalline white. Irretrievable. The ice might easily break. Unless the wind carries it away, or snow covers it, someone will notice it and they're bound to think that a girl must have drowned in the lake this spring. They'll search for a hole in the ice, and when they find none, they'll say: "A hat proves nothing!" The sun was low in the sky now, the sky was overcast, and when I kissed her, her mouth tasted of spring-water and pasteurised butter. We walked back down, sliding on the steep slopes. Toboggans in the snow.

The young receptionist had thought we must have got lost. Rosa gave him back his sunglasses, but he swore on his mother's head that he wouldn't take them back. The weekend was over. We promised him we'd be back. His name is Akli and his face was puffy with swelling pustules of acne. It was obvious he couldn't stop picking at them.

8

I've just got a letter from Rosa. She's living in the Lebanon. She says she's doing alright. I'm happy for her. Truly. Ramdane, too, has left. They went together. I've no alternative now but to get back together with Chabha, my wife. She moved in with her parents more than a month ago. They think I'm away working. A month without sending word, that's a bit long. Basically, I do love her, Chabha. I miss her. And the kids.

Hereafter

It's weird, but I wasn't even scared for one second when they came for me! I heard their hesitant steps on the dark corridor outside and I knew that this time, it was me they were coming for. They were walking quietly so as not to wake the others. I reckon the rules tell them to do that. If an inmate ever managed to shout out when they came to get him, they gagged him and dragged him down to the underground courtyard at the double. I'd only just hear his last muffled screams, my ear pressed against the door, holding my breath.

I wasn't kept waiting long – just three months, I think. I'd got used to my cell and the gross smells from the tiny hole I used for a toilet. Complaining would have been pointless. Nobody would have listened. But in spite of everything, I was very lucky! Some went totally crazy, waiting for long years on end for the fateful dawn. Me, I passed my time thinking of Samia and of the sea. I was determined to stay healthy, in body and in mind, for the execution. After all, it was *my* execution, the only one I was ever going to have!

They were all very kind. The public prosecutor offered me a cigarette. I smoked it down to the filter. I knew I wouldn't be getting another drag for a while. Then the imam came to ask me to recite the chahada. He looked serious and fiddled nervously with a handsome string of green beads. As soon as he'd finished with me, two brutes crashed me backwards against an upright girder set in the ground and tied me to it with a rope that smelled of burning. The soldiers in the platoon lifted their weapons – not

27

very tidily – and fired! The brutes fell, struck down. One bullet went through my thigh, another lodged in my stomach, and a third did for my left eye. I was mad with joy. None had hit my heart. Not one. I was going to point this out to them, but some imbecile came and finished me off with a bullet in my neck. So I decided to keep quiet.

The next day, it was raining torrents when I saw the imam again, in the cemetery. He was wearing a black raincoat over his white gandoura. I recognized him straight away. My cousin Mourad was sticking close to him. I still owed Mourad money. I was glad to see that he'd come to my funeral. I knew he wasn't the type to bear a grudge over such a small sum. He'd shaved his moustache and had my smartest suit on.

Practically all of them were there: Baba-Sliman's son-in-law, Boualem, the village policeman's son, Kadour, Samia's father, Si-Larbi. Even Kaci-Tampouce, whose bike I'd stolen when we were kids, was there. I'd tears in my right eye to see them weeping for me so sincerely and turning back every ten yards as they walked away, at the risk of cricking their necks.

But what rotten luck after all! I'm so sad I could die. Nobody says anything here. They all act like they're dead and buried.

Mama

1

We had a long wait before the general and his entourage arrived. Men in suits chatted in the shade of a skeletal olive tree, the only tree on the square.

– Fifty coffins… fifty medals. That's the count.

– And your speech?

– In my pocket!

Chairs had been arranged facing the municipal offices. The first row, reserved for the army officers, was empty. Two policemen walked up and down and signalled to us and the others to take our seats. "You've been waiting all these years, be patient a little longer!" Old men in turbans and old women in veils protested against the heat. Youngsters smiled in satisfaction at the thought that their fortunes were about to change.

– Apparently the president himself gave the order!

– The president is coming?

– What?

– No, but he's given the order.

– Wallah?!

– Ah!

I looked across one more time at the soldiers in parade uniform flanking the line of coffins, and plonked myself in a chair on the back row, far from the television cameras.

Everything had been ready since early that morning. The table with its multicoloured cloth stood on a podium which had been borrowed from the village school and set up at the edge of a thorny field adjacent to the town hall. A pile of small green boxes hid the microphone. The sound technician's repeated "one-two, one-two" echoed through the mountains, "one-two, one-two".

I'd taken the coach to Aïn Nachfa and continued on foot. As I came into the village, one of the policemen on duty signalled me to stop. I lifted my arms so he could carry out the usual frisking. And after I showed him my printed invitation and my identity papers, he told me where the ceremony was taking place.

– Follow the tarmac road and turn right by the fountain. The wali, the mayor and the commissioner are there already.

– Thank you.

A little further on, I was accosted by a man wearing a green ribbon on his left shoulder. He introduced me to three men in suits standing under the shade of an olive tree. "He's from Algiers," he said.

The wali, the mayor and the police commissioner looked amazingly similar. They all had the same dull look in their eyes and the same rebellious paunch. "So, you've come from Algiers," repeated the wali. Or it might have been the mayor. Or the commissioner. I said I nearly hadn't come at all because of the insurgents' roadblocks and so on. The man with the ribbon came up, with someone new in tow. With a "Salam oua'âlikoum!" I took my leave of the wali, the mayor, the commissioner, the man with the ribbon and the new man, and went off to sit down.

The inscription on the huge banner hanging from the façade of the town hall read: To The Glory Of Our Martyrs. It was only attached at one end. What if it falls down, I wondered. A gust of wind and it would blow away over the thorny field. And then they'd never get it back. But the deputy mayor, on overdrive, had already spotted the risk and shrewdly shouted out: "Shift your arses and get that fixed!" Three, four, five local constables began running in all directions.

The general arrived at three in the afternoon. The cameras shuddered.

All along the line of coffins, the soldiers stood to attention. I stubbed out my cigarette, then everything happened very fast.

"We have built you motorways! Alge…, sqvtx…, crac…, quack!" The general wore dark glasses. His lips moved too fast. I stopped listening. My head span. My stomach hurt and I felt a mad desire to piss. I forced myself not to throw up on the spot. Eventually I relieved myself twenty metres away by the side of the tarmac road.

When I came back the mayor or the wali or the commissioner was speaking. We were called up and one by one we were handed our bronze medals engraved with the national emblem, in memory of our relatives whose remains had been found, buried less than three feet below the surface, by a local shepherd's dog.

The general's car sped off in a cloud of dust in the wake of the escort squad and two armoured personnel carriers, followed by the television truck. The wali, the mayor and the commissioner vanished. The sun was a bloody red and the crickets were screaming.

2

From her bed, Mama can hardly see the sun when it sets behind the grey blocks. In order to see it sink into the sea it's necessary to get out of bed, descend the indoor staircase two steps at a time, cross the ground-floor corridor, open the door, slide down a four hundred metre slope and take the shortcut along ruelle de Gargotiers to get to the boulevard. But to see the sea, all you need to do is go up onto the roof-terrace. It's only twelve steps to climb.

Mama hasn't moved for ages. She desires no more than to wait for the moment when the sun passes in front of our small, badly positioned dormer window, before it disappears behind the watchtowers of Barbarossa Prison. That always seems to liven her up a little. Her lips tremble and stretch. One would think she was starting to smile. She says nothing. She's said nothing for too long. She may even have forgotten that the sun sets in the sea.

Twelve steps up, my little end of a roof-terrace, my territory. It overlooks the bay and the port where the sleeping city's futile dreams come to drown themselves. I smoke a cigarette, my head wreathed in stars, and drink in the fresh breeze pushing the rows of clean laundry. When I was a kid I mainly used to come here in order to cry in peace. Hot tears, often enough. There was no lack of reasons. My pigeons would open their tiny eyes wide and rock their heads like a clock's pendulum. They answered my sobs with endless cooing.

Some used to say: "That littlun's got a heart of stone." The teacher in the first year of school put me at the back of the class among the dunces, because she was always asking what my father did. And I never wrote anything on the form. She pulled my ears, pinched my cheeks, and mostly she hit my fingers or my head with her stick of olive wood. But I didn't cry. She knew very well that my father was long dead. I'd wait till I got back home and then I'd go up onto the roof-terrace.

One day she called me to her office and announced she'd decided I could sit at the front. As a bonus she gave me a mint sweet and a credit point. All because I'd started a rumour that my uncle was an officer.

I ate the sweet in the break and swapped the point for a piece of gruyere. And when Mama heard about this, she gave me a good hiding, and went to cry by the windowsill of our dormer.

So I told the teacher that my uncle was not an officer, nor a businessman, even adding that he spent most of his time after work playing dominos at the corner café.

Years went by and I never moved from the back of the class. But by now I was no longer that kid who'd swap credit points for pieces of gruyere. And Mama by now was stuck in the bed, waiting for the sun to pass by our small, badly positioned dormer window before it sinks behind the grey blocks of the abattoirs opposite.

Mama never had time to talk to me about my father. Apparently a bullet killed him, striking him right in the heart. She'd plenty else to think about. She was too busy cleaning people's houses. I went to sleep to the humming of the sewing machine. And anyway, I didn't really understand. The teacher knew that my father had died in the war. She asked me to recite my nine times table. The most difficult one... Nine sevens, sixty-three... I didn't get a credit point. No point, no gruyere. The commissioner's son got two. He's an ass. He sits by the stove. At the back of the class it's cold. The teacher's not a whore but she sits the rich men's sons near the stove so they won't catch cold. Mama made me a hankie out of her old dress. The teacher has holes in her tights. She's too thin and her perfume smells of onions. My uncle bought me a nice fountain pen when I was in year six. He even gave me fifty dinars. I went swimming with my friends from the neighbourhood at the beach called 'Foot of the Wall', where all the drains in Algiers run out. There was no sign saying anything like 'No bathing'. And even if there had been, I'd still have gone for a dive, or two. My heart was warm. To me, summer meant too many things that we should have, but didn't have.

Algiers, the naked! I didn't recognise her, she'd become so provocative. Her underwear was on view now. And the good citizens had already laid out their ambitions for everyone to see. Their children's rosy cheeks contrasted with our excessive pallor. We had ended up catching cholera. And Mama, Mama, who could no longer see the sun pass across our small dormer window, just before it sank into the sea, must never know.

Bus Story

I've often walked past the regional administrative centre. Never stopped. Or only to catch my breath or tie my laces. I've always thought there wouldn't be much to see from inside. On the south side, the windows are kept shut, or occasionally they're opened onto thick grey curtains. On the north side, the windows are kept wide open to catch the breeze which comes directly from over the sea, without mingling with the suburban noise and stench. But now and then, piercing screams produced by the children of the nearby neighbourhoods, who were keen visitors to the public gardens just a stone's throw from the imposing edifice, spoiled everything. It was as if they deliberately meant to remind the occupants of the fabulous offices on the top storey that nothing can be taken for granted. The public gardens were put under an exclusion order, and order was thereby restored.

"The bigwigs like to meditate in the dark. Their underlings avoid disturbing them, for fear of getting on the wrong end of their flashes of inspiration. And since it all goes on so long, they end up unable to see. 'S logical," said Ammi-Ouali, known as "the oldie", withdrawn from circulation one scorching day by the back wheel of a bus which had chosen the wrong moment to skid on the skin of a local banana.

Busses still climb the road alongside the regional administrative centre. Their tyres are still worn away by the fuming tarmac. Passengers look one another in the whites of the eyes. Very interesting things can be observed there. Heads turn away, eyes are put in pockets. You breathe, you wait.

– There should be different busses for women and for men.

– And one for kids.

– And one for your mother.

– Got any snuff?

– I don't do snuff.

– Stuff snuff!

Nobody bothers looking over towards the public gardens. The benches are empty. No lovers now to spy on. No lovers to condemn or to envy. Nothing but pigeons waiting for the night, waiting to sleep.

Rendez-vous

Ali was quite content with his brief encounters with Fatima. They had got into the habit of meeting at the end of the day in a fallow field, halfway between the village and the barracks. The tall, dense grass protected them from the curious and inquisitorial eyes of the villagers, who were viscerally hostile to any such assignations. In order to get there, Fatima had to pretend to be visiting her cousin at the far end of the village. And he, dodging the surveillance of the guardroom, scaled the walls topped with barbed wire and shards of glass which enclosed the military zone.

The warrant officer had said: "A soldier who never deserts is not a true soldier. But if you get caught, beware!" And Fatima certainly deserved the sacrifice of a shaved head and close arrest.

"We'll get married!" Ali had murmured to her, the first time he had managed to steal a kiss. She had wept that day, and he had realized that he loved her as he had never loved anyone.

In Algiers, where his uncle had brought him in to help in his bakery shop, long before he had received the call-up to do his military service, Ali had made up his mind to look down on the city girls: "Slags!" Indeed, several times he'd paid the price in mockery from insolent grammar school girls who laughed right in his face at him. They thought he looked most amusing in his all-white shop-boy's outfit, as he delivered huge desserts to the customers. Some even tried to make a pass at him. "The world's turned upside-down!" he would grimace. Back home, out in the sticks, he had told his friends about the frivolous urbanites:

"Nothing at all like our families' modest daughters, who'd never even dare to raise their eyes to look at a man!"

And then came the army. He had to leave his family once again. The day he left, his mother blew her nose on the sleeve of her dress, she had cried so much, but afterwards she comforted herself with the thought that her son was going to do his duty as a man. She had not forgotten to make him galettes stuffed with dates, his favourite when he was little. Standing at the doorway of her shack, she followed him with her eyes until he was just a tiny dot, far down the road, thought for a moment of her dead husband, and disappeared in turn, banging the zinc door.

Ali had planned to build a "solid" house after finishing his military service. To clear their plot of land for crops. To marry. He liked Fatima. She was pretty, she was gentle, she could not fail to make an ideal wife. He should talk to his mother about her on his next leave. Meanwhile, Ali and Fatima continued to meet secretly. And, unable to contain such a great love, their outpourings became more daring. "We'll get married," Ali murmured to her. And finally, they abandoned themselves to each other. Now nothing was what it had been before. Everything had toppled over into a world without constraints or prohibitions. What did they care for the human beehive! All the buzzing had ceased, as if by magic. Now there was only the rustling of dead leaves under the weight of their entwined bodies.

Stretched out on the luxuriant grass, Ali contemplated the sun as it set majestically behind the hills. Fatima ought to have been here by now. The evening before they had said: "Till tomorrow!" And: "As always!"

But what an atrocious pain was seizing his stomach now. A blunt pain, a pain which left him winded. He felt the ground reel beneath his feet. Coming round, he was stretched out face down on the ground, his hand stuck to his stomach. He tried to call out but could only emit a long, unintelligible groan, raucous and jerky. Then he tried to move, increasing the pain which wounded him in the depths of his guts. But the wind, as it seemed, gently lifted him and turned him on his back.

The blood had at first spurted like a geyser. The others continued to hack at his body with their knives.

Ali was waiting for Fatima. He was even a little early. Then the others came, who knows where from, and leapt on him. The blades pierced his khaki jacket and fine off-duty uniform, the next to last button flew off. They had shouted: "Go to hell, where your tart's waiting for you!" But Ali was no longer listening. He was waiting for Fatima, who was late, but who was surely going to come.

Over in the barracks, the line-up was one short that evening. "Ali Ghrib!" shouted the sergeant a second time. He took the tiny pencil, wedged the register against his chest, made a large cross and continued the roll-call, a fixed grimace on the corners of his fleshy lips.

Local Therapy

Contrary to meteorological prognostications, the weather was superb.

Omar stretched feverishly, cracked his ten fingers one after the other, as if in a spirit of revenge (this habit used to earn him his schoolteachers' enraged admonishments and punishments), then considered the furtive trails of white cloud following one another in single file and disappearing behind the dead angle of his window.

"I'm a bird!" Omar told himself as he slid out of bed at the same time as his shadow. He went straight to the bathroom and inadvertently turned on the tap. A flood of creepy crawlies, the same ones that haunted him by night, filled the basin. He turned the tap off again and one-two-three, on tip-toe, crossed the twenty tiles which separated him from his bed.

Strange whisperings, punctuated by sudden shouts and the sound of breaking glass, emanated from the large lizard on the ceiling. Car-horns had taken over from the morning cooing of the pigeons. The streets had been invaded by a curiously silent crowd, utterly timorous due to the lack of interrogations. Bodies misshapen by virtue of reason bowed very low to the scarecrows placed here and there on the pavements and actually went down on all fours when occasional dignitaries passed by hidden behind dark glasses and smoked-glass windows.

"Before the dignitaries belch into the microphones," sighed Omar, "they stuff themselves. Patriotically! Just to make sure that the rest of humanity can't guess the dish of the day in time." And he watched them as they lied, without batting an eyelid, all down through the generations.

"The rest of humanity's just a clapometer!" Omar told his shadow, who was indifferently munching the piece of nougat which had dropped, the night before, from the pocket of the matron on guard. Omar had had more than one opportunity to kill her. He certainly would have, if she hadn't been so pretty. And it wasn't the daily injection of phenobarbital which stopped him. All was still clear in his mind. Despite the lobotomy which he'd been subjected to on the very day he was admitted. The doctor in charge had said: "That makes one less quibbler!"

The drill had left practically no scar. It might have been a beauty spot on his forehead. Over the years, three long hairs had sprouted around it. Three years, three hairs. The equation of his internal clock.

He did sometimes bang his head on the walls, or on the bars on the window, for the ticking had become unbearable. "Wild beasts in cages kill themselves that way, apparently," his shadow always pointed out.

Omar had to calm down once and for all. The instructions were clear. "Double the dose of creepy crawlies, triple it! No more tinkering about!" the doctor ordered. The matron on guard obeyed. Omar cried: "I'm a bird!"

Two tugs were sticking to the sides of a cargo ship returning to port. In the evening, the television had announced bad weather for the following day.

Of Stars and Men

1

Some imagine that the world is upside-down and aim to set it upright. One utopia more or less won't make any difference...? They tend to fall on their faces, being fixed upon the stars. And yet they remain as lovely as ever, with their heads covered in wounds, their faces full of stigmata. But time, fraying at the pace of the sufferings of passers-by, scorches their hearts and crushes their huge eyes. Might they then, perhaps, doubt a little? So what! So long as there are stars and men.

2

I know not what miracle has kept the cretins from impersonating us too at their masked ball every day, what miracle has kept us from joining the cast of the puppet show. Was Nietzsche not wrong in claiming that "all small things are innocent of their smallness"?

Eyes wither quickly if you don't watch out. Hearts rot the moment you compromise with mediocrity. If you can hear a melody amid the din, it's because you've succeeded in taming the sun of your childhood. The heart which is heeled over by the winds of legend.

Khobzists, Khobzism

If prostitution is the oldest profession, "khobzism"[5] must be the oldest doctrine in the world. No one is born a "khobzist", nor must one be a graduate of Harvard or Bab-Ezzouar in order to become one. The essential thing is to be able to conjugate the verb "to eat" in every language, in every mode and in every tense.

The gist of the "khobzist" catechism is: "If you eat and if he eats, then I eat too!" Nothing could be simpler. And given that certain people's hunger is wolfish, chronic, is indeed (so to speak) generative, we shouldn't be surprised that they make a feast of every last thing they can get their teeth into. Never mind the flavour! So they never miss a festivity. And above all memorial galas!

However, you mustn't suppose that anarchy reigns around the groaning board. Oh no! A quasi-military hierarchy is in place: "Tell me what you eat and I'll tell you who you are." And since the pathways of "khobzism" are often impenetrable, low-ranking "khobzists" apply their own criteria, those of force: always best. To make the task easier, there's never been a shortage of wire brushes[6], even on days of public celebration or mourning.

---

[5] "Khobzism", from the Arabic for bread, is used in Algeria to refer to opportunists.

[6] The "wire brushes" refer to the idiomatic use of "brosser", meaning to flatter.

"Khobzism" henceforth deserves to be cracked up as having a truly socio-philosophical dimension, worthy of the spirit of this dawn of a new century. We, the intelligentsia, will take on this task with gaiety in our hearts, lending our stomachs to its success. Then we'll be able to write in big clear letters on the blackboards in our infant schools: "To eat or not eat, that is the question!"

The Sham

The sham is an artificial flower placed in a crystal vase among expensive ornaments and history books.

One may be detained by the sight of it, still as lovely as ever, eternal spring, while everything around us inexorably grows old.

But as soon as one steps closer to it, its petals form the fixed smile which the dead sometimes have, their eyes wide open onto nothingness.

Put out the lights!

Then you will smell the naphthalene.

The Poet's Garden

In a country where business fever was spreading at the speed of sound, carried by the mysterious world-wide "*hafmorstuff*" virus, one poet still believed in beauty and the sublime values of the simple life. He had chosen to isolate himself on the roof-terrace of a high-rise apartment block, where he lived in an old washroom, three metres by two, perched above the city, happily contemplating the splendid sunrises and sunsets.

Happily, until one day an uncommon idea entered his head: to convert this aerial-infested, otherwise uninhabited space into a pretty little garden. But this was impossible, as he was well aware. He brushed the ludicrous idea away. Yet he failed to appreciate the power of his utopia. For he could not get out of his mind the image of a garden as lovely as those of ancient Babylon, hanging over a city which once had been beautiful, now made unbearably ugly by its inhabitants.

And so he came to know the agonies of insomnia, the terrible lassitude of endless days and nights. "If only I could get hold of a plot of land far from the city! That would be so much easier!" he thought to himself. And in an excess of optimism he went to consult the city council.

He knocked on many doors which stayed shut, indeed double locked, and waited many entire days in icy corridors, till he caught a bad cold, but always he got the same response: Lots of money! Dozens and dozens of millions! And worse still: at least ten years on the waiting list.

Blowing his nose quietly, so as not to disturb the other people waiting at the bus station, he ruminated on his dreams and frustrations. An hour later he felt the crowd carry him to the back of a bus. His dreams jumped off and his frustrations, stronger than ever, tugged at his baggy clothes and his sagging skin, making him look quite pitiful. All around, squashed bodies talked and talked. And a moment later he saw them turn into a flock of sheep and goats, bleating away.

"Baaa!" said the pretty goat opposite. "Baaa! Baaa!" replied her friend. He felt an insane urge to bleat as well. He went: "Baaa!" The crowd fell silent. Some stared. The gentle little poet burst out laughing.

That night he decided not to bother with permission from the city council, since they seemed to be allergic to any idea coming from outside their own circle of brains.

Over the following days, the residents of his district noticed that their neighbour was unusually agitated. The more reserved called him bizarre; others, as always, called him mad. He was busily filling big bags with soil to pour onto the terrace. There was a week of coming and going. Then he bought seeds and set about sowing them in a geometrical pattern with a symbolic meaning known only to him. Nobody cared what he was up to with all this soil. "A poet's whim!" said some.

Years went by. People ambled in the streets. Housewives scrutinized shop windows and kids played cops and robbers. They had all forgotten the poet's very existence.

Then came the day when Sidi-El-Hadj El-Thawri raised his head even higher than usual as he thanked god for the blessing of a broad-shouldered son-in-law. His youngest daughter had just married an army colonel three times her age, previously married and with seven children, after picking him up at an eventful evening do. "A daughter worthy of her father!" he was thinking complacently, when he froze, not daring to believe his eyes. But by the time he'd rubbed them he knew it was real: there really was a garden high over the building. Recovering from his stupor, he ran for the nearest police station to notify the authorities.

"A garden! A dreadful garden! May I go blind, inshallah, if I tell a lie!" cried Sidi-El-Hadj. At first, the officer sitting behind his huge desk took him for crazy. But finally he agreed to send a patrol to investigate.

Disappointed by this lack of urgency, Sidi-El-Hadj decided to take matters into his own hands. "No need to bother my son-in-law over such a little thing! We can mete out our own justice!" And he went to inform the neighbourhood committee, of which he was the leading member.

An immense crowd gathered to stare at the strange sight. Gigantic flowers reached out from the roof-terrace, hanging over the void. Not just flowers but shrubs and enormous green plants. No one could ignore it. Something had to be done!

People's eyes were filled with something like horror – and perplexity. In worried tones they whispered to one another about the weird man living up there like a savage. "A garden on top of a block of flats! A scandal!" "Roof terraces aren't for growing flowers! Television aerials, or maybe a game of football or a bit of jogging. But a garden!" "Utter madness! Exhibitionism!"

All present felt a growing sense of imminent danger and of deepening unity in their shared hostility to the poet, and they devised ever more insulting terms for him.

"A garden! Where?" cried a sophisticated lady who was driving by in a luxury car. "That's all we need! A garden hanging over our heads!" She'd speak to her husband, a senior civil servant. "He'll take steps!"

Meanwhile a man had been cleaning her superb car's windscreen with a rag, and as she drove off at high speed, she flung him into the ditch without even noticing him. The rag landed on his battered face. There was no pulse. He was dead. That did it! Sidi-El-Hadj solemnly proclaimed: "May his soul be with god. He died working, he'll go to paradise." "It's all that poet's fault!" cried a man with a massive paunch. "That's right!" shouted the crowd. "Send the young boys home, there's gonna be a ruckus!" shouted fat-belly, but the young boys wouldn't go.

"Let's all go up there and get him," ordered Sidi-El-Hadj.

The little poet had heard the noise of the crowd but had assumed that it was just another of those rows which had grown so common since the general spread of *hafmorstuff*. However, when the noise carried on, he decided to take a look. Seeing a multitude of faces looking up, he automatically turned his own head to look above. But there was nothing to see up there but the radiant blue spring morning sky.

56

"Kill him! Kill him!" roared thousands of voices. The sight of him enflamed their ferocity and they raced for the entrance to the building. The poet recoiled in fear. Meanwhile Sidi-El-Hadj, propelled by the crowd, slipped on an orange peel and fell, hitting his head on the pavement such that his soul instantly departed from his body, fleeing at the rate of several light-years in a few seconds, only to end up squashed into a gigantic black hole. That really did it now! The sons and all those of the tribe of Sidi-El-Hadj chanted "Death! Death!"

Now rewards were offered. Si-Mokhtar, the richest shop-keeper in the neighbourhood, promised five million. Still richer, Ammi-Madani, a notorious "businessman", offered ten million to whoever could reach the terrace first and throw the poet off it.

Men fought to get up there and gain this patriotic honour. Two more died, three were seriously injured by being trampled, and two disappeared, according to the boys who had scaled the nearby trees in order to survey the situation. Further deaths and injuries occurred as the mob ascended the stairways, but the majority lived to swarm out onto the roof-terrace.

The little poet was sitting at the foot of a willow tree, his back to the crowd, looking straight ahead. For a moment, all fell silent, following his look. But there was nothing to be seen – just the line of a horizon that remained rather distant. There was a heavy silence, eventually disturbed when a fat fly stung the bleeding head of one of the wounded.

"Kill!" shouted a son of Sidi-El-Hadj, and they all fell on the poet, grabbed a part of him, and hurled him into the void.

The poet fell, fell. Some thought he took much too much time over it. Others used the word miracle. Some leaned over to get a better view, only to fall themselves and be instantly splattered. And still the poet fell.

The garden was sublime. There were flowers of every colour and every possible shape. Nothing like it had ever been seen. One by one, the poet's attackers turned from the spectacle of his fall to admire the splendours of his garden. Lovers opportunistically picked roses, while the elders dug up shrubs.

Alerted belatedly, the minister of the interior arrived, panting, with his fifty-strong bodyguard. "We'll see – Don't touch anything! We'll see what we'll do about this garden! Trust me!" His arrival had shut the crowd up, and they spent the next quarter of an hour acclaiming him. He seemed put out that he had not had time to prepare a speech.

"First of all, we shall give this garden a name," he improvised. "Let it be known from now on as the Sidi-El-Hadj Garden, in memory of that saintly man." Another quarter of an hour of acclamation followed. "And now, everybody go home quietly!" barked a plain-clothes policeman brandishing a gun.

The days following the incident were absolutely calm. The men went about their daily occupations with a sense of having done their duty, with light hearts and heads held high. The housewives gathered outside chic shop windows and talked and talked. And the young boys played at being the little poet.

The Voice of Reason

In the early days he shut it all out. He wielded his pen like a Kalashnikov, targeting anything he found suspect. It was beyond him how people could get so fat, so stupid, so nasty, so quickly. He trained his fire point blank on all those who had, as he put it, "sold off the autumn leaves to the highest bidding wind" (referring here no doubt to the ideals of the revolution of November 1954, which in his view had been betrayed by an outlaw elite). Alwach Dopp was intoxicated with the exhilaration he felt every time he produced another dynamite article, and he slept deeply, dreaming of better tomorrows.

Each morning he faced up to dull realities, eager to extract from them the fuel that fed his rage. But at the *Gentle Citizen*, the journalists had long since given up writing. They merely transcribed or, mostly, put their names to press releases spat out by the teleprinters. The rest of the time they spent swelling the queues outside the grocery stores.

He, though, always obstinate, kept knocking on the editor's door, hoping that one day his voice might become a fixture (this the measure of his revolt) at the heart of the newspaper where he had been working for ten years. On the obituaries!

Although Alwach Dopp was a gentle man (like all the journalists on the *Gentle Citizen*), he finally flipped. One day he had a subversive idea, and carried it out at once: he reversed the hierarchical order of the obituaries. But it was spotted in time and he had to do the work all over again. The entire staff on the newspaper knew that only the intervention of a childhood friend, a high-ranking officer, had saved him.

And while the sun continued shining as low as ever over the whole country, his colleagues carried on putting their names to press releases spat out by the teleprinter, having transcribed them in their entirety. Nobody bought the *Gentle Citizen* now anyway, and hadn't done for ages, except for the various administrative institutions of the state which were obliged to take at least a thousand copies a day on subscription.

The queues outside the grocery stores grew longer, ever longer. And Alwach Dopp, as dazed as an amateur boxer in the tenth round, became besotted with Fahma, a pretty girl who was determined to inculcate in him the rudiments of ambition. He put up faint resistance, let down his guard and promptly received a charming crocheting hook on the chin (fatal).

Since that day he has heard nothing but the birdies' cheep-cheep, swears only on the lives of his children, mechanically transcribes and puts his name to the press releases spat out by the teleprinters at the *Gentle Citizen*.

Criticisers and the Criticisable

On political manners in Algeria

There was a time when Criticisers were infinitely more numerous than the Criticisable. And so, in order to cease being a minority, the latter suggested to a hand-picked selection of the former that they should become Criticisable.

Having performed their self-criticism, the Criticisers in question thanked the Criticisable for thinking of them and chorused that they had long aspired to become Criticisable, but only destiny and habit had made them into Criticisers.

Seeing their ranks swell, the Criticisable turned deaf ears to the increasingly acerbic criticisms of the vast mass of Criticisers. Until the day when a number of them were actually lynched by desperate Criticisers. Then they realized that in order to guarantee their future and that of their children, they must remain, of course, Criticisable, but do so whilst criticising the Criticisable. So they became Criticisable-critical Criticisables. The Criticisers were left reeling, unable to tell true Criticisables from false Criticisers...

Adel Guemar - Biography

Soleïman Adel Guémar is about the same age as the independent republic of Algeria. He worked as a freelance investigative journalist from 1991 until 2002, when he claimed political asylum in the UK . Adel's stories, like his poetry, have "a fighter's edge, a tough beauty." (Lisa Appignanesi). They address the agonies of contemporary Algeria and the survival, despite everything, of dreams of a different world. His political poems are published in "State of Emergency" (Arc Publications, 2007), in French with English translations by Tom Cheesman and John Goodby.

Palewell Press

Palewell Press is an independent publisher handling poetry, fiction and non-fiction with a focus on books that foster Justice, Equality and Sustainability.

The Editor can be reached on enquiries@palewellpress.co.uk